W9-APR-959

Little Hands
Creative STICKER Play

ROBOTS

First edition for the United States, its territories and dependencies, and Canada published in 2014 by Barron's Educational Series, Inc.

Text, design, and illustration © copyright 2014 by Carlton Books Ltd.

All inquiries should be addressed to:
Barron's Educational Series, Inc.
250 Wireless Boulevard
Hauppauge, NY 11788
www.barronseduc.com

ISBN: 978-1-4380-0536-2

Author: Mandy Archer
Design: Andy Archer
Illustrator: Tom Woolley
Senior Art Editor: Emily Clarke
Senior Editor: Anna Brett
Production: Ena Matagic

Date of Manufacture: April 2014
Manufactured by: Leo Paper, Heshan, China

Product conforms to all applicable CPSC and CPSIA 2008 standards. No lead or phthalate hazard.

Printed in China
9 8 7 6 5 4 3 2 1

BARRON'S

Metal madness!

Say a happy hello to the robots — the nicest bunch of nuts and bolts you could ever meet! Give each one a sticker gadget to hold.

Annie-Droid, pleased to meet you!

Beep, beep! I'm Ratchet!

Rover has a toy cat called Felix. He could pop up anywhere in this book. Flip through the pages. Can you find Felix four times?

Boots bungle

Sparky has lost his favorite footwear! Fill the shelves with shoes, then stick on Sparky's white rocket boots.

Annie's checklist

Annie-Droid is packing her robot toolkit, ready to go to work. Can you stick in all of the items on her list?

Check list

1. Wrench

2. Screwdriver

3. Hammer

4. Drill

5. Pliers

Find the stickers in the middle of the book.

Space robots

These high-tech robots are orbiting through space.
Use stickers to connect each one to the mother ship.

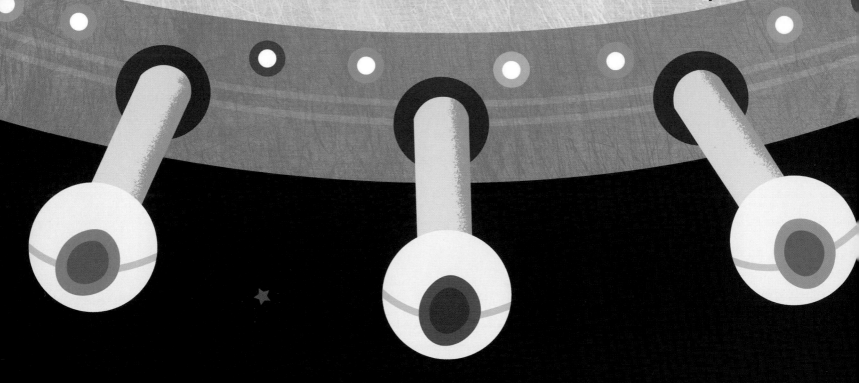

Malfunction!

Ratchet has suffered a computer error! Study the blueprint at the top, then use your stickers to correct the bottom image.

ANSWERS ON PAGE 64

Loony lab

This science lab has been taken over by robots!
Use your stickers to add more wacky science expirments.

9

Plug problem

The gang need to recharge, but their cables are all messed up! Who has put a plug in first? Fill the fastest robot's battery with power bars.

ANSWER ON PAGE 64

Look at the line

Look at the robots rolling off the production line. Which one isn't a perfect match? Use your stickers to make this robot right again.

Eureka!

Annie-Droid is working on some crazy new inventions!
Choose your favorite objects from the sticker pages,
then put them onto the graph paper.

Wacky welding

Find the stickers in the middle of the book.

13

This chrome crew are welding a new machine together. Stick safety goggles onto each robot, then add some extra sparks.

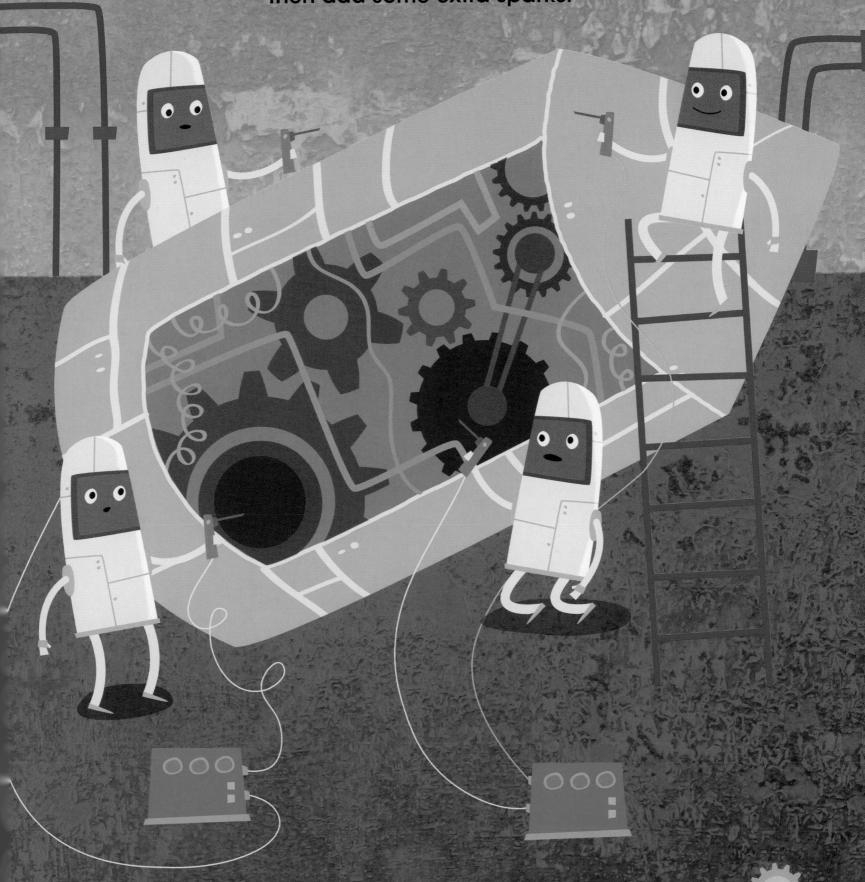

What's your I.D.?

Study the picture clues, then stick the correct robot at the bottom of each chain.

Find the stickers in the middle of the book.

14

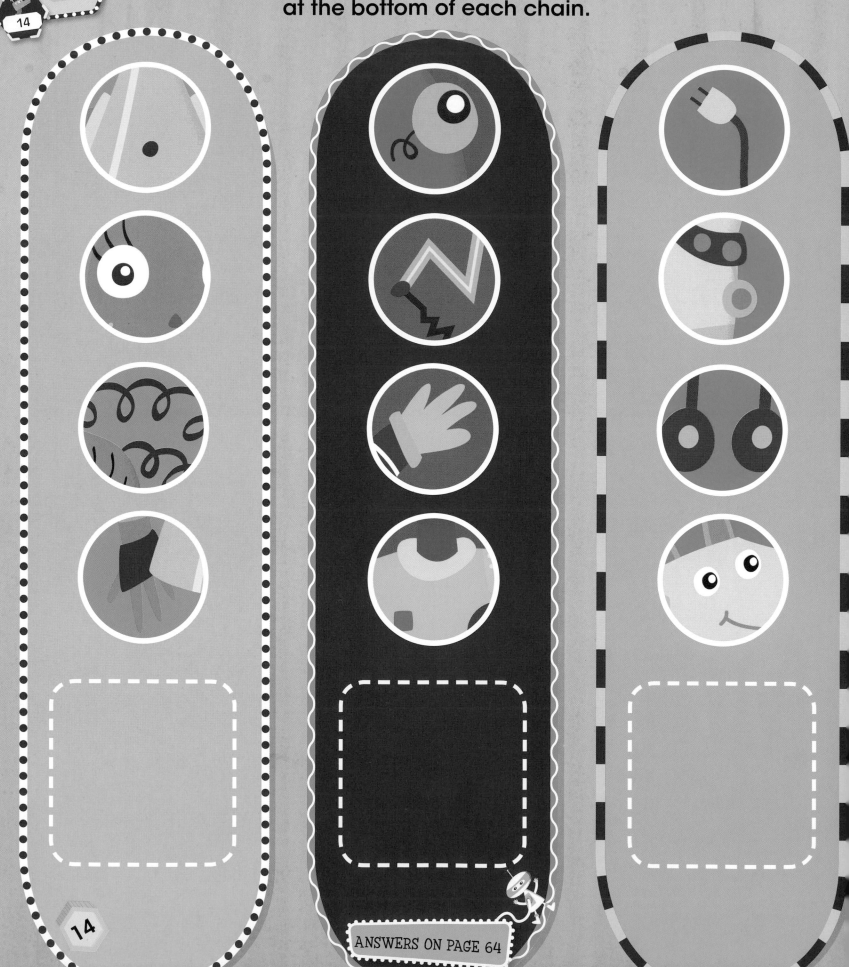

14

Button trouble

Annie fancies a metal makeover! Stick new buttons on her shiny chrome tummy.

You could add other stickers, too.

Nuts and bolts

Rachet is sorting out his tool kit. Can you find the matching nut for each bolt? When you've finished, add more robot tools to his box.

16

ANSWERS ON PAGE 64

Smart and shiny

Sparky, Rover, and Ratchet are getting ready for a picnic in the park. They want to look their very best! Give each one some smart robot accessories.

Futuristic fun

All the robots are wired up and ready to start the picnic! Decorate the rug with yummy robot snacks — nuts, bolts, and oil cans!

Tote away the trash

After the picnic, this eco robot collects the trash and crushes it flat. Read the labels and then put the right items into its trash cans.

Metal trash

Batteries and oil

Food waste

Build a buddy

Find the stickers in the middle of the book.

21

Rover wants a friend! Use stickers to build a robot pal for him to play with. What will you call the new pet?

You can make more than one buddy!

21

Roll on, Ratchet!

Ratchet needs to get across this busy street to pick up his wrench. Stick in a trail of arrows for him to follow.

Find the stickers in the middle of the book.

ANSWER ON PAGE 64

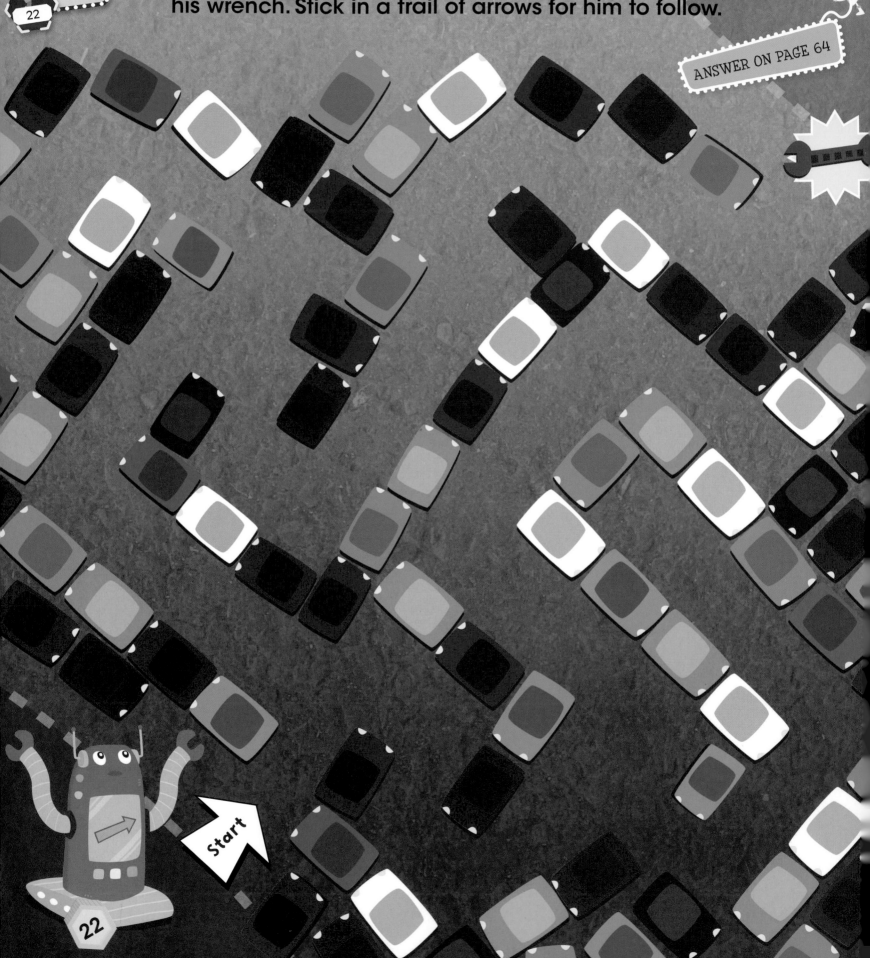

Start

Silly Snaps

Find the stickers in the middle of the book.

Rover and Sparky are playing in the park. Use your stickers to make the bottom picture match the top one.

Lunar landing

Our robots have touched down on a strange new planet!
Stick in a robot flag, then add the aliens that live there.

Robot races

Which robot is the speediest? You decide!
Stick on trophies and flowers.

Sparky's Spruce up

Sparky needs some urgent maintenance work!
Stick in some tools to help Annie get the job done.

Find the stickers in the middle of the book.

Screwdriver Search

Annie-Droid has lost six screwdrivers in her sleep capsule.
Stick a matching screwdriver over each one when you find it.

ANSWERS ON PAGE 64

What's the point?

Can you build a new robot using only triangle-shaped parts? Give it a try!

Find the stickers in the middle of the book.

29

Roller robots

These robots would get around town much quicker if they had wheels! Stick a slick set onto each machine.

Find the stickers in the middle of the book.

32

Back to work

Ratchet's always on the go! He's zooming around the science lab today. Stick in the missing jigsaw pieces to complete the picture.

ANSWERS ON PAGE 64

Silly screens

How is Ratchet feeling today? Choose a mood face, then stick it onto the computer screen on his tummy.

Flying robots

The sky is filled with robots whizzing left and right!
Stick in a hoverboard for each one to ride on.

Crazy cake

Annie wants to make a cake for her cousin Zelda.
Can you help her by building a crazy metal cake?

Cyber city

Annie-Droid has arrived in the city to deliver Zelda's cake. Which path will lead her through the skyscrapers? Stick Zelda at the end of the correct path.

A

B

C

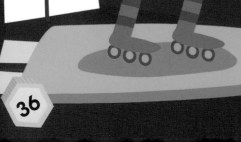

ANSWER ON PAGE 64

Find the stickers in the middle of the book.

Charge me up!

This tired little robot has used up his battery. Stick in a new one, then light up his head with colorful bulbs.

Robot hotel

Look who's checking into this space-age hotel!
Use your stickers to decorate Sparky's bed spread.

Bot-time story

Sparky always runs a story through his processor before he goes to bed. Put in picture stickers to complete this tale and give it a happy ending.

Once upon a time a robot called ☐ and his dog ☐ were walking in the city. They saw a ☐ , sticking out of the ground.

A ☐ popped his head out. He explained that the ☐ had broken down.

☐ radioed his pal ☐ . The robots used their ☐ to fix the broken ☐ . The ☐ was thrilled. Well done ☐ ! The End.

Tidy the tools

Ratchet normally has seven blue wrenches in his workshop. Can you hang them on his shelf?

Find the stickers in the middle of the book.

Factory fun

Every morning, Sparky and his friends go to work at the inventions factory. Use your stickers to fill the floor with robots, gadgets, and gizmos.

Find the stickers in the middle of the book.

42–43

Lights out!

There's been a power cut in the science lab.
Stick the right robot over each shadow.

Find the stickers in the middle of the book.

44

ANSWERS ON PAGE 64

High-tech kennel

Rover's kennel is futuristic and fun! Decorate the inside with computer screens, buttons, and flashing lights.

Find the stickers in the middle of the book.

45

Add antennae

Annie-Droid's buddies have lost their antennae!
Stick a new one on each robot head.

Find the stickers in the middle of the book.

Rows of robots

Look at these brand new toy robots packed up in their boxes. There's one missing from every row. Can you stick the right robot into each line?

Find the stickers in the middle of the book.

1

 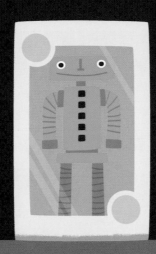   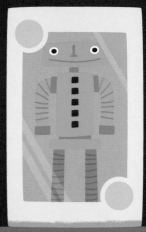

2

3

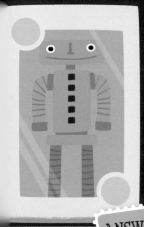    

ANSWERS ON PAGE 64

Find the stickers in the middle of the book.

Testing times

These shiny robots are flying a spaceship. Use your stickers to complete the tasks set by mission control.

Control panel

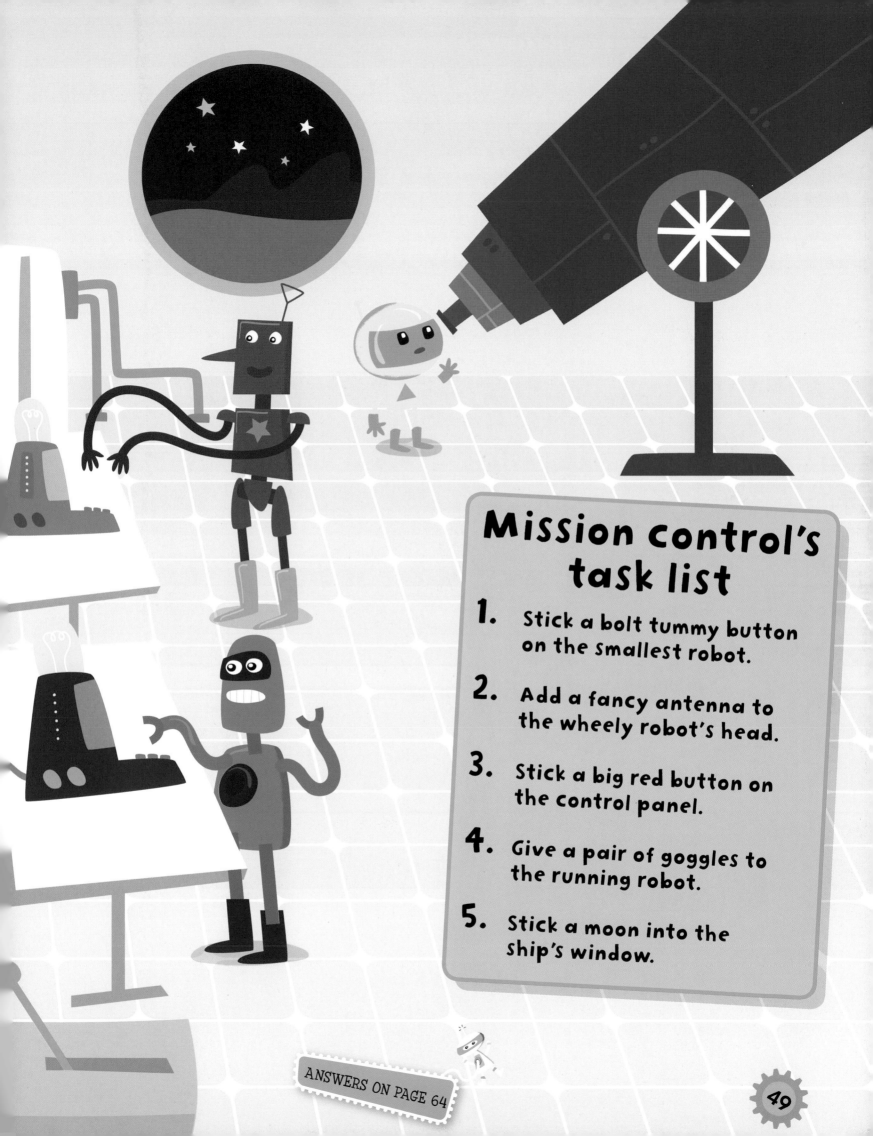

Mission control's task list

1. Stick a bolt tummy button on the smallest robot.

2. Add a fancy antenna to the wheely robot's head.

3. Stick a big red button on the control panel.

4. Give a pair of goggles to the running robot.

5. Stick a moon into the ship's window.

ANSWERS ON PAGE 64

Crash and bash!

This robot comes with a bionic bashing arm. Find five metal fingers on the sticker sheet, then put them in place.

Sparky's sudoku

Find the stickers in the middle of the book.

Sparky wants to fill this computer screen with pictures of his friends. Can you help? Make sure that each robot only appears once in each column, row, and mini-grid.

ANSWER ON PAGE 64

51

electric dreams

Find the stickers in the middle of the book.

What do robots dream about at night? Read the thought bubbles, then stick the correct picture over each one.

A brand new tool kit

A soothing oil bath

Racing in space

A game of chase

ANSWERS ON PAGE 64

Robot vision

What can Sparky see through his new super specs?
Use your stickers to decide!

You can add other stickers, too.

53

Screen Scene

These computers aren't working properly. Stick bright new pictures onto their flickering screens.

Locked lab

Poor Rover can't get back into the lab! Match the keys to their shapes on the shelf, then find the right one to fit the door.

Find the stickers in the middle of the book.

55

Let's do the robot!

Ratchet, Annie, and Sparky have been invited to a funky robot disco! Decorate the room, then add some dancing droids.

Find the stickers in the middle of the book.

56-57

Find the stickers in the middle of the book.

58

True or false?

Are you a robot expert? Let's find out! Stick a picture of Sparky next to each true statement and a danger sign next to each false one.

	True	False
1. Rover is a robot hamster.	☐	☐
2. Annie has pink hair.	☐	☐
3. Sparky has one red leg and one purple one.	☐	☐
4. Robots need power to make them go.	☐	☐
5. Ratchet rolls around on wheels.	☐	☐
6. Annie has wheels on her boots.	☐	☐

58

ANSWERS ON PAGE 64

At your service

What has this robot butler brought you? Fill his tray up with tempting sticker treats!

Annie's attachments

Annie-Droid has all sorts of handy attachments to bolt on when she needs to. Use the stickers to try a few for size.

Big day out

How many customers are lining up to get into the robot theme park? Put a sticker ticket next to the right number.

9

8

6

ANSWER ON PAGE 64

Find the stickers in the middle of the book.
62–63

Whiz, whirr, and peep!

Ratchet, Sparky, and Annie love riding on roller coasters! Stick in the missing track, then fill the park with more happy robots.

Answers

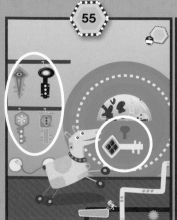

You can find Felix four times in this book on pages 8, 29, 46 and 54.